HAZEL TOWNSON

RUMPUS ON THE ROOF

Illustrated by David McKee

Andersen Press · London

First published in 1995 by
Andersen Press Limited,
20 Vauxhall Bridge Road, London SW1V 2SA

British Library Cataloguing in Publication Data is available
ISBN 0–86264–591–3

Phototypeset by Intype, London
Printed and bound in Great Britain by the Guernsey Press Company Limited,
Guernsey, Channel Islands

Contents

*For the pupils of Bury Grammar School
Preparatory Department, who have shown
such enthusiasm for books.*

1

Dad Mourns the Absence of a Hero

'That can't be our Harry!' cried Jim Bunch, dropping his luggage on the doorstep in shock. 'Why, the lad's nothing but a skeleton! Haven't you been feeding him, or what?'

'That's a fine way to greet the boy after all this time!' Mrs Bunch sprang to her son's defence. 'Skeleton, indeed! He's not always stuffing himself with junk food, if that's what you mean. Our Harry eats a proper sensible diet, just right for his age.'

'Well, all I can say is, if he eats any more of his proper sensible diet he'll disappear altogether.'

Mr Bunch strode indignantly into the

house, annoyed at this hitch to his home-
coming. He had just spent two whole years
abroad, helping to build a dam in very hot
and difficult circumstances. Surely that had
entitled him to a hero's welcome, befitting a

man with muscles the size of hand-grenades and a tan like treacle toffee?

'Better get you built up, my lad!' he threatened Harry darkly. 'Jogging, press-ups, good steak dinners and regular sessions down the gym, that's what you need. Good job I came home when I did.'

Harry's stomach shuddered. He didn't want to get built up. He was perfectly happy the way he was. Besides, all that time spent exercising would be time lost to his hobby of photography. Harry was the youngest member of the local Camera Club and had already won two prizes. His life's ambition was to become a photo-journalist following in the steps of such worthies as Lord Snowdon.

'And I bet top-liners like him don't waste their time on joggings, gyms and press-ups,' Harry thought rebelliously.

Harry's mum gave her son a reassuring wink behind Dad's back.

'Don't you worry, son!' that wink said. 'Just leave your dad to me. I'll make short work of this fitness phobia.'

No doubt she would have done, too. But unfortunately Harry's gran was taken ill that very night with something called a stroke, causing Mrs Bunch to dash off to Leeds first thing the next morning to look after her.

'Don't know when I'll be back. Expect me when you see me!' declared Mum, distractedly stuffing clothes into a suitcase.

Harry thought a stroke sounded a very gentle sort of illness, hardly more than a mere touch of something, which could be sorted out in no time at all, but his mother assured him that it was nothing of the kind. A stroke could leave Gran paralysed for a while all down one side of her body. She might even need nursing for weeks.

'Lucky your dad came home when he did.'

'Lucky for some!' thought Harry bitterly. He and his dad would now be left alone in the house together for a pretty long stretch and he was already dreading it.

'Fate moves in mysterious ways,' Dad declared cheerfully as he rolled up his sleeves and set about grilling a couple of thick steaks for lunch. 'Now we can really set the ball rolling. For a start, I can supervise your diet myself, get you filled out into something fit to look at.'

'I don't eat steak,' Harry informed him quietly. 'I'm a vegetarian.'

'A vegetarian?' Mr Bunch swung round from the oven. He couldn't have looked more dismayed if Harry had admitted to being a serial killer. 'What sort of nonsense is that supposed to be?'

'It isn't nonsense. I just don't believe in eating animals.'

Mr Bunch peered suspiciously at his son. 'Your mother's put you up to this, hasn't she? She always was daft about animals,' he growled, shooing the cat from the kitchen with the side of his slipper.

'No; Mum's not a vegetarian. But she doesn't mind me being one. She says I'm entitled to my principles. She cooks two separate dinners.' In wistful reminiscence Harry added: 'She makes me some super vegetable pies with flaky pastry, or sometimes she does butter-bean casserole or Ohio stewed corn.'

'Stewed corn?' Dad repeated in horror. 'I can't believe I'm hearing this! What sort of a meal is that for a growing lad? Anyway, you needn't think I'm going to mess about with separate meals. You'll eat what you're given, and like it. As for principles, I'll bet you don't even know the meaning of the word.'

'But, Dad – !'

'I'm not going to argue. You just get that down you!' Dad slapped the steaks on to a couple of plates and added a mountain of oven-warmed chips.

'I don't eat chips, either,' murmured Harry. 'They're bad for you.'

Mr Bunch's face reddened beneath his tan. He looked as though he were about to ignite, but fortunately the situation was saved by the doorbell. Harry sprang thankfully to answer it. He hated arguments, and even the smell of chips was enough to turn him queasy. After only a few seconds he reappeared in the kitchen doorway.

'It's my friend Rashid. He's come to collect me for lunch at his house. Rashid's a vegetarian as well. Cheerio, Dad! See you later!'

'You just come back here! Your food's on the plate!' shouted Mr Bunch. But it was too late; the front door had slammed and the boys were already halfway up the street.

'You'll catch it now!' Rashid grinned cheerfully, knowing Mr Bunch's reputation.

But at that moment Harry didn't care. Retribution was far away in the future. At least he'd escaped the steak and chips.

Harry stayed at Rashid's house all day and kept on postponing his departure. Each time he glanced at the clock he decided: 'I'll just have another half an hour.'

In the end Rashid's mother had to remind Harry that it was getting on for bedtime and his dad would be starting to worry.

'We don't want him to think we've kidnapped you!'

Luckily, Dad was fast asleep in front of the television when Harry reached home, so he was able to sneak off to bed unnoticed. But if Harry Bunch thought he had escaped unpunished he was wrong.

2

Harry Hides in the Hedge

Next morning, Harry was roused disgustingly early.

'Wakey-wakey! Beautiful morning! Just right for a run across the common.'

Mr Bunch wrenched open the bedroom curtains and Harry groaned.

'Dad, it's school holidays.'

'All the more reason to start our jogging programme. Come on, now; let's have you out of bed! We don't want any stewed-corn wimps in our family.'

Dad wrestled the duvet into submission at the foot of the bed and seized Harry's arms.

Ten minutes later, the two of them were dressed for action. Harry stood miserably on the doorstep, dreading the next half-hour. He didn't mind running at his own speed and on his own terms, but he had no wish to be bullied into a breathless wreck by his father. He could foresee disaster with such clarity that he almost flopped down there and then in a defeated heap. Yet once again he was saved by the bell! Just as they were about to set off, the telephone rang. Mr Bunch went to answer it, realised the call was going to take some time, and urged Harry to start off without him.

'I'll soon catch you up!' he promised confidently, turning back to the telephone with a notepad at the ready.

In a sudden surge of elation Harry recognised his chance. Now he need jog no further than the end of their path, where he could scramble through a well-known hole in the privet and hide in next door's garden. Once he had seen his dad start off, Harry could then sneak back into the house (making sure he looked suitably travel-stained) and be waiting there gasping for breath, pretending he'd finished the course in record time. Dad ought to be pleased!

No sooner thought than done! Quick as a curse, Harry darted through the bushes and curled himself up among the somewhat prickly vegetation in old Mrs Lathom's wild, untended garden. That garden was a wonderful place to hide. The grass was at least a metre high round roses which had all run wild. Besides, Mrs Lathom was a bit of a recluse who never seemed to have any visitors, apart from Harry himself who ran errands and did little jobs for her from time to time. The lad could have hidden there for a week without ever being discovered.

Mind you, it was not very comfortable. Quite apart from the prickles, the grass was still wet with dew and there was actually a big, fat slug trailing slimily along right in front of Harry's nose.

Yet something happened which promptly took his mind off his discomfort. Two men appeared at Mrs Lathom's garden gate. Harry could just see their feet and legs through the gate bars. One was wearing jeans and trainers; the other had navy

trousers – obviously part of a good-quality suit – and black, shiny shoes. They didn't open the gate, but stood there, talking quietly. Yet not quietly enough; Harry could hear their conversation quite plainly.

'Well now, this is the house I told you about, Norm!' Trainers pointed out eagerly. 'The one with the old woman living on her own. Must be eighty if she's a day. No relatives, no visitors to speak of.'

'You sure?'

'I should be! I spent long enough checking it out.'

'H'm! Let's have a look, then, Dez.'

Harry froze. Had he stumbled across a couple of would-be burglars, casing the joint?

There was a pause while Norm stepped back to survey the roof of the house. Then, to Harry's amazement, another kind of villainy came to light.

'Only one slate missing, far as I can see.'

'Soon remedy that, though, won't we?' Dez replied gleefully. 'Get the ladder up, crack a few more slates, rip a few out. Before she knows it, rain'll be pouring in. She'll be begging us to mend it.'

'How do we know she'll pay up?'

'No problem. She may be an Old Age Pensioner, but she's not poor. See them candlesticks in the window? Solid silver, they are. Bet the old place is full of suchlike stuff, all valuable antiques.'

'Antiques are no good if you can't persuade her to sell 'em. We'd be a lot better off with a mattress stuffed with fivers.'

'Well, you never know your luck. Anyway, I do know she's got a bank account. I saw her there the other day, drawing some money out.'

Harry lay listening in dismay. It didn't take a genius to realise by now that these men were confidence tricksters. They obviously intended to come back later when Mrs Lathom was up and about. They would persuade the old lady to pay an enormous sum to have her roof repaired . . . after they had wrecked it in the first place. Ten to one they wouldn't even do the repairs properly, either. In fact, they might ask for the money in advance, then disappear without doing any repairs at all. Harry remembered that old Mrs Graham up the road had once had a similar experience. She had paid a hundred pounds to have her fence mended, and all the workmen had done was to knock in a couple of nails before disappearing with the money.

Harry felt angry. Mrs Lathom was a nice enough old lady who did not deserve to be tricked. She had never done any harm to anyone; in fact she had been particularly good to Harry. She might be a bit forgetful sometimes, but she always remembered Harry's birthday; better still, she let him browse for hours among her late husband's photograph albums. (Mr Lathom had been a founder-member of the Camera Club. In fact, he was the one who had introduced Harry to the hobby in the first place, and Harry had even inherited one of his cameras when he died.) It was unthinkable to let any harm come to Mrs Lathom, so Harry felt it was now up to him to protect her from these villains.

How could he do it? So absorbed was Harry in desperate rescue plans that he did not hear his dad sneaking up behind him until it was too late.

'Caught you!' Mr Bunch's arm grabbed Harry's shoulder from behind and began to drag him out of the bushes. 'Clever – but not clever enough! Next time you pick a hiding place, don't leave so many telltale footprints.'

Mr Bunch began to frog-march his son towards the gate.

'So you thought I'd set off jogging without you, eh? I'm not daft, you know! I can guess what sort of tricks an out-of-condition lad like you might get up to.'

There was no point in protesting; Harry was well and truly caught. He did consider telling his dad about the confidence trick-sters, but decided he wouldn't be believed. Dad would think such a tale was merely an excuse to escape the fitness programme. He was cross enough already.

'You may as well know,' declared Mr Bunch, 'that I don't like that sort of under-

hand behaviour; you have to learn to face up to life. So I'm going to teach you a lesson. Apart from jogging with me – which you have *not* escaped – you're grounded for the day. Once we get back, you don't go any further than that garden gate. Understand?'

'But, Dad, it's Camera Club tonight.'

'Ring up and cancel it.'

'It's already paid for. Mum pays for ten sessions in advance. You learn a lot at these sessions, Dad. You pick up some really good tips. Mum won't be pleased if I miss it.'

'Well, you'll have to tell her you've picked up two even better tips today, then. First tip – "Face up to your challenges instead of chickening out." And second tip – "Never pay for anything in advance; you might drop dead." Believe me, those two gems of wisdom will stand you in better stead than all the photography lessons in the world.'

Harry was furious. He had never missed a Camera Club session before. They were the highlights of his life and he now considered his day to be totally ruined. As if that wasn't disappointment enough, he had meant to go round to Rashid's that afternoon. Rashid's uncle had promised to reveal the secrets of the Indian rope trick. Now, instead of these two most desirable treats, Harry would be reduced to mooching round the garden by himself.

Suddenly he had an idea. If he was grounded, then at least he would be on the spot to observe the second act in next door's drama. Just suppose he had one of his cameras at the ready . . .?

3

The Villains Catch a Spy

In the middle of the morning, while Harry was stretched out on his lawn still recovering from a severe case of jogging, Norm and Dez came back, as the lad had guessed they would. This time they drove up in a battered grey van with balding tyres which proclaimed itself to belong to RITEAWAY ROOF REPAIRS. As proof for all to see, a rusty metal extending-ladder rattled loosely on the roof-rack.

Tired or not, Harry was instantly alert. He immediately grabbed his Instamatic camera – which he had left ready in the hall – and concealed himself in the bushes again, ready to observe everything that happened. First of all he directed his lens through a gap in the undergrowth and took a picture of the van, clearly showing the registration number. Then he lay low, straining his ears to pick up anything that was said.

The two men briefly checked over their original plans.

'Let *me* do all the talking!' Norm insisted. 'You look after the practical side of things.'

So then Dez very practically propped himself up against the side of the van and lit a cigarette, while Norm, the well-dressed one, walked smartly up the path and rang Mrs Lathom's doorbell. When the old lady answered it he turned on all the charm he could muster, which included raising his hat, performing an exaggerated half-bow and producing with a flourish a printed business card. However, he took care to whip this away again before Mrs Lathom had had time to look at it properly.

Harry strained his ears to catch every word as Norm began to speak very earnestly to the old lady. Was Madam the owner of the property? Had she looked at the roof

lately? Did she know it was extremely unsafe? Was she insured against accident? Suppose the milkman or the postman, or even a cherished visitor, were to be injured by falling debris . . .?

From his hiding place Harry watched the consternation grow on Mrs Lathom's face. This had obviously come as a great shock to her. She probably hadn't looked up at the roof for years, if ever.

At last the old lady followed Norm down the garden and into the street. There they were joined by Dez, and the three of them stood on the pavement gazing up at the offending roof.

'I can't see much wrong with it,' protested the old lady timidly. 'Of course, my eyesight isn't what it was.'

'Takes more than a casual glance. It needs a professional eye with years of experience behind it. From down here you can't even see all the slates – a lot of which are broken – and under them slates are beams, and them beams are far from healthy. I mean! You've only to look at your roof-ridge!'

'Yeah, see that saggy bit in the middle?'

'And the way the chimney-pot's started to lean?'

'Frame's rotted on your skylight, too.'

'Yes; that'll need replacing for a start. And if that's gone, you can bet your life there's worse to follow underneath.'

First Norm, then Dez, pointed out various non-existent structural deficiencies, solemnly shaking their heads. Mrs Lathom's manner grew more and more distressed.

'Well, I don't know what to say . . .'

'Can't say anything till we know for certain, me dear! Got to check our facts. Best if we let Dez here put the ladder up and take a proper look. Then we can give you a full report and an estimate of what it'll cost to put things right.'

'Oh, I don't know . . .' began Mrs Lathom.

'No, 'course you don't, me love!' Norm cut in hastily. 'You're all confused. This has come as a bit of a shock. But in a way this is your lucky day. Because if we hadn't come along, you'd have been in for an even worse shock soon enough.'

Mrs Lathom shuddered.

'But now you *know*, you can soon have things put right,' Norm went on cheerily. 'If you didn't, you'd be worrying yourself to death about it. Am I right? You'd be lying awake night after night, listening for the bad

weather to start up, storms and blizzards and gales and I-don't-know-what . . .' With an eloquent shrug of his shoulders Norm felt there was no need to say any more.

'Well, I suppose . . .'

Norm gave the old lady a quick pat of approval. 'That's the spirit! A trouble faced is a trouble halved, that's what I always say.' Turning to Dez, he added: 'Get the ladder up, then, while we go in and have a little discussion.' With heavy hints about cups of tea for the workers, Norm led his victim into the house and firmly closed the door.

By this time Harry had acquired several pictures of the two men. He thought these could be used as evidence that they had visited the house, but would that be enough? He really needed much more definite proof of their intended fraud. Now, if only he'd had a tape-recorder as well as a camera . . .!

Dez had now unstrapped the ladder from the van and was carrying it up to the house. He manoeuvred it noisily into place and was just about to mount it when down there in the bushes a frog leapt on to Harry's crouching back. Harry didn't mind frogs as a rule, but this one had taken him completely by surprise. Moreover, it had moved so fast that he wasn't even sure it *was* a frog. Merely glimpsed from the corner of his eye, it could have been something much worse. Harry leapt to his feet, shaking himself violently to get rid of the creature. This frenzied activity sent him crashing from the bushes into Mrs Lathom's garden, gasping with shock.

Hearing the commotion, Dez swung round and was almost as startled as Harry.

'Hey! What're *you* doing here?'

'I – er – I live next door!'

'You've been spying, haven't you?'

Dez abandoned the ladder and started hurrying purposefully in Harry's direction. That lad had a camera slung round his neck. Suppose he'd taken some pictures? Worse still, suppose he'd overheard? Well, Norm would have to know about this. Norm would want to ask the lad a few questions. It was more than Dez's job was worth to let the boy get away.

'Come here!' yelled Dez in a thoroughly

menacing voice. He streaked across the garden at top speed and was almost within grabbing distance of Harry when Harry turned and ran. Grounded or not, the lad flew out of Mrs Lathom's gate and off towards the common at almost the speed of light. Dez, growing puce with effort, chased after him.

Mr Bunch would have been proud of the way Harry ran. The lad reached the common in record time and darted in among the first clump of trees he saw, casting anxious backward glances at his pursuer. Alas! Those backward glances meant that Harry was not looking where he was going. All of a sudden he careered right into a girl who was just about to emerge from the trees.

'Hey! Watch it!'

'Sorry!' Harry lost his balance and almost came a cropper, but the girl caught him round the middle and stopped him from falling.

'What's your hurry, then?'

'Quick! Let me go – I'm being chased!'

'Well, in that case you need to disappear,'

decided the girl, dragging him towards a cave-like opening in a high bank of earth well-hidden by the surrounding trees. Before Harry realised what was happening, he found himself in a dark, earthy passage.

4

A Girl Comes to the Rescue

The girl said her name was Petra and that Harry could go home with her and lie low for a while.

'Best thing to do if you're being chased.'

'But I've got to get back as well. I've got to sort something out. It's urgent.'

'Well, you can't have it both ways. If you're running away, you can't run back yet. You've got to give it time – stands to reason.'

The passage soon emerged on the edge of a clearing in which there was an old-fashioned caravan painted in interesting colours – a Romany caravan, Harry realised in surprise. Nearby, a horse was grazing.

'This is where I live,' said Petra, pointing

out her family as well as the caravan. Her mother was hanging out washing; two young brothers were engaged in a friendly fight, and her dad was sitting on a stool by an open fire, mending an umbrella.

'That's my dad's job,' explained Petra. 'He's really good at it. He goes around looking for broken umbrellas that people have thrown away (you'd be surprised how many you can find, especially on a windy day) then he mends them and sells them again.'

Harry marvelled at this ingenious way to earn a living, and hoped he could think of something equally original when the need arose. With a last backward glance he followed Petra into the caravan, confident by now that he really had given Dez the slip.

Petra had been watching Harry closely to see how he reacted to her home and family. Some of the 'friends' she brought here turned decidedly cool when they saw how she lived. But Harry didn't seem to care. Perhaps he had too much on his mind to notice? Better find out what he'd been up to!

'Well, now that I've taken the trouble to rescue you,' began Petra, directing Harry to a comfortable window-seat, 'I think I deserve to know why you were being chased.'

Sturdy young Petra, who had often been chased herself for one bit of mischief or another, was beginning to feel quite protective towards this undersized boy who was nowhere near as big as she was, though probably older. As for Harry, he was only too grateful for the rescue. Over a mug of herb tea (which was a great improvement on his dad's black brew) Harry began to tell the tale of Mrs Lathom's roof. He even showed Petra the pictures from his Instamatic camera, but the girl was unimpressed by these.

'If you're thinking of going to the police, you'll never prove anything with those.'

'I know!' agreed Harry miserably.

'What you want is a photo of the roof before they touch it. A really clear photo that proves the roof's in good repair. If you can show that to the old lady she won't pay these villains any money, then your problem's solved.'

Harry said nothing, but sat deep in thought.

'Well, come on, then! You can't sit here day-dreaming. You need to get that picture now, while they're still busy chasing after you. We'll have thrown them off the scent by this time.' Petra reminded Harry that he had said the ladder was in place, so it would be an easy matter to climb it and take a really good photograph of the roof.

Harry's brain suddenly sprang to life. Climb that great, high, rickety builder's ladder? Right up to the roof? He hadn't much of a head for heights and the thought of such a climb set his stomach lurching. Besides, as he now explained to Petra, only one of the men was chasing after him, and even he had probably given up by now. The other man was right there on the spot.

'I'd be bound to be caught.'

'Not if I distract their attention,' the girl grinned. 'I could get the pair of them right out of your way.'

'I don't think that's a good idea. Didn't anybody ever warn you not to speak to strangers? Those two are villains. You don't know what they might do.'

Petra grinned wickedly. 'I don't have to speak to them. They don't even need to see me. There's plenty of ways of distracting people's attention if you know how. Anyway, I can be a villain too, when I like. I once stopped a policeman from arresting our Jimmy, and in the middle of our last campsite campaign I climbed up the front of the Town Hall and hung a banner from the top balcony saying TRAVELLERS ARE PEOPLE!'

'In that case,' retorted Harry quickly, 'since you're the one with the climbing experience, why don't *you* go up the ladder and take the photograph?'

He hadn't really meant it, for he didn't take the ladder idea seriously at all. But to Harry's amazement Petra accepted the challenge.

'All right!' she decided without hesitation. 'It's a good cause, and I will! But you'll have to get rid of those two for me. Here's what you do . . .'

There was obviously no time to be lost, so even as Petra was explaining her plan, the two of them started straight back to Mrs Lathom's garden, Harry's chief worry being whether or not he could trust Petra with his precious camera. The ladder was still in place, but to Harry's relief there was no sign of the two men. The van had also disappeared, and Harry wondered if Dez had come back for it in order to ride round looking for him.

'Norm might still be in the house, though, trying to persuade Mrs Lathom to part with her money.'

'Only one way to find out,' said Petra. 'Ring the doorbell. But hand me your camera first, then I can shin up the ladder as soon as you give the all-clear. Thumbs-up if he's not there, okay?'

'I told you – we're not supposed to speak to strangers.'

Petra sighed impatiently. 'You're not going to. Just ring the bell, then dart away and hide, and see if he comes to the door.

If it's the old lady who comes, you can ask her if he's there. Use your brains!'

This girl was very bossy. Still, Harry guessed she was younger than him, and he was beginning to feel uncomfortable at letting her climb the ladder and do his detective work for him. His dad must be right after all; he *was* a wimp, though he hadn't realised it until this moment. Even worse, he was sure that no amount of body-building would help the situation. It was all in the mind. Feeling suddenly depressed, Harry rang the doorbell.

Mrs Lathom usually took a long time to answer the door as she was slow on her feet. But today so much time passed that Harry guessed the old lady was either out, asleep or dead. He peered in at the windows but could see no sign of life. The only clue, draped over the back of a chair, was the shawl which the old lady usually wore across her shoulders when indoors. At last he called to Petra: 'I think they've gone out.'

'He's probably driven her round to the bank to get some money,' decided Petra.

'Well, let's not waste our chance. Here goes!'

Agile as a monkey, she began to shin up the ladder with the camera strapped round her neck. Harry ran to hold the ladder steady. It was the least he could do, he thought, as he stared breathlessly up towards the retreating figure of his new friend. He could not help admiring the girl's courage, while feeling shamefacedly grateful that it was she and not himself up there. He felt he could no more have climbed to the top of that ladder than he could have flown. Yes; after all his dad was right to refer to him scornfully as a stewed-corn wimp! That must be what Petra thought as well. Standing there at the foot of the ladder, Harry could suddenly see himself as others saw him, and it was not a pretty sight.

When Petra reached the top of the ladder she was quick to note that, apart from one missing slate, the roof was in good condition as Harry had claimed. Moreover, the skylight frame was as sound as a millionaire's bank-balance, and the chimney stood as straight as a Grenadier guard. It would make a reassuring photograph. Unfortunately, when poised on the topmost rung of the ladder Petra was not in a suitable position to get the picture she wanted. What she needed was to be able to step away from the wall a little bit. She began looking around for a better vantage point.

Then Petra noticed that the front bedroom had a bay window, the top of which was flat, with a small stone parapet round the edge. Fearlessly, she made a giant stride across on to this and stepped clear of the ladder, clutching the guttering for support. Great! Now she could move to the outer edge of the bay and take exactly the picture she wanted. Excitedly, she raised the camera to her eye.

This was the moment at which Jim Bunch caught sight of his son from a bedroom window and rushed angrily out of the house.

'I thought I told you you were grounded?' yelled Harry's dad as he sped out of his own garden gate and in at Mrs Lathom's, only to find one crime close on the heels of another.

'And what do you think you're doing hanging on to that ladder? Just about to climb it, weren't you? Well, it's lucky for you I caught you in time or you might have broken your neck. Have you *no* sense?' Mr Bunch was now fiercely angry with his son, yet just as angry with a person or persons unknown. 'People have no business leaving ladders where kids can get at them. Irresponsible idiots! It's just asking for trouble.'

Jim Bunch remembered clearly that as a boy he had been fascinated by ladders himself and on one occasion had almost had a nasty accident. The memory of it was still frighteningly vivid.

Before Harry realised what was happening, his dad had seized the offending ladder, dragged it away from the wall and lowered it to the lawn.

5

Petra Gets Stranded on the Roof

Harry's dad frog-marched Harry back home, quelling all the lad's attempts to speak.

'Dad, there's somebody . . .'

'I don't want to hear any excuses, so you can just keep quiet!'

'But, Dad – !'

'One more word and you'll be grounded for the rest of the holidays without any spends. I can find you plenty of housework to do.'

It was obvious that Mr Bunch had not spotted Petra, who had flung herself down flat on top of the bay when she saw him coming. But now the poor girl was trapped up there without the ladder, and at any minute the two villains would be back. Horrifying possibilities chased one another through Harry's imagination as he tried desperately but in vain to get a word in edgeways.

Goodness only knew what might have happened if once again the situation had not been saved by the telephone. This time it was Mrs Bunch, ringing to ask her husband to send on to her urgently by the next post something which she had forgotten to take to her mother's. This involved Mr Bunch in having to find, wrap and post the item in a great hurry to catch the next collection. Abandoning Harry in the house with dire threats as to what would happen if he left it, Dad at last rushed off to the post office with the parcel.

One last chance! As soon as Mr Bunch had gone, Harry flew back into next door's garden. Jumping up and down to get a better view, he realised he could see no sign of Petra. Surely she couldn't have fallen? Perhaps she was lying injured somewhere? Or perhaps she was just too scared to move?

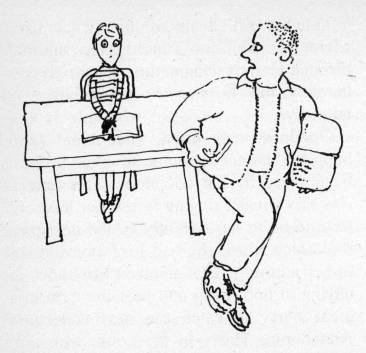

Whatever had happened, it was all his fault. Sick with worry, Harry realised that the only thing he could do was to go up and look for her . . . and he must do it *now* before he had time to think and frighten himself to death.

It was not easy for a skimpy lad like him to raise the heavy ladder or to guide it to the right place on the wall. Once, swaying dangerously, the ladder nearly fell back on top of Harry, but he just managed to redirect it in time, and eventually set it in place against the wall, more or less where it had been before. Then came the hard bit. Sweating profusely, Harry took a deep breath, gritted his teeth and began to climb. It was the bravest thing he had ever done – and probably the most foolhardy.

Five – six – seven – Harry counted the rungs as he went up. He knew he must not look down, and once or twice he even closed his eyes, swaying precariously on the ladder. Ten – eleven – twelve – how many rungs did this ladder have? Perhaps it was a mistake to be counting them in the first place.

When he reached fourteen his foot slipped. Clinging desperately to the sides of the ladder, he hung there for several seconds with one foot waving wildly in the air and the other slithering helplessly about on the fourteenth rung. This was it, he thought. Now he would be sure to fall, and his remains would be splattered all over Mrs Lathom's concrete path. In total panic he made all kinds of rash promises to whatever

gods might be listening. He would do anything, eat anything, renounce anything, be
grounded for life, if only he were allowed to
survive.

Well, it seemed as if his prayers were answered, for suddenly and amazingly Harry found himself at the top of the ladder. There was the roof, sloping sickeningly up in front of him. And there, on his right-hand side, lying flat on top of the bedroom bay window behind a little parapet of stone, was Petra.

'You're still alive!' marvelled Harry, casting a brief scared glance in her direction. 'I couldn't see you from the ground, so I thought . . .'

''Course I'm alive, idiot! I just had the sense to lie low. Now let's get back down to earth, double quick! You go down a few steps, then give me a hand so I can get back on the ladder!'

Petra rose carefully to her feet and stretched out one arm towards Harry. But evidently the ladder was not quite in the same place as before. The distance from the bay window to the ladder had increased. Petra might still have tackled the gap, if only Harry could have been relied on for strong support. But he looked so nervous that she suggested it would be better if he went back

down the ladder again and moved it closer
to the bay window.

'M-move the ladder?' repeated Harry,
trying desperately to keep calm. By some

miracle, he had managed to climb to the top of that ladder once, but he felt sure he would never be able to do it a second time. Then he made his fatal mistake. He looked down.

Harry could never remember what happened after that. Petra said he swayed and she thought he was going to fall, so she leaned out as far as she could to help him. In his panic he caught hold of the camera which Petra still wore on a strap round her neck and nearly pulled both of them to their deaths. But somehow Petra hung on, clinging to a drainpipe with one arm and grabbing Harry by the scruff of the sweatshirt with the other. Slowly and painfully she managed to drag Harry over the parapet and on to the top of the bay window with her. Harry flopped face down at Petra's feet as, with a last desperate kick, he sent the ladder crashing to the ground.

6

Harry Offers a Thin Chance of Escape

Norm drove Mrs Lathom home from the bank in his van, feeling pleased with his morning's work. The old lady had been persuaded to draw out some cash, and now there were definite prospects of financial rewards!

As they walked towards the house Norm noticed the fallen ladder, but assumed that Dez had moved it and had then gone off to look for refreshments. Pretty typical, that would be; Dez spent more time on refreshments than anything else.

Norm had asked for five hundred pounds as an initial sum to pay for the materials required, but Mrs Lathom had only been able to withdraw two hundred and fifty pounds in cash. The rest would have to be by cheque. She sighed as she sat down to write the cheque now, knowing that there would be very little money left in her account; hardly enough for any future emergency. Still, it couldn't be helped; she had to have a sound roof over her head.

The girl at the bank had helpfully put the money into an envelope, and Mrs Lathom was just about to hand this over, together with the cheque she had written, when the doorbell rang. It was Mr Bunch, enquiring after his son.

'Harry's supposed to be grounded, but he's gone missing again (third time today!) and I thought he might have come back here, since I've already caught him in your garden once, playing about on your workman's ladder.'

Norm looked up sharply at this, and Mr Bunch launched into a tirade against leaving dangerous ladders lying about untended.

Norm replied with some equally nasty comments about unruly kids who were allowed to do just as they liked with no vestige of parental discipline. Kids who wrecked and vandalised other people's property and showed no respect for old ladies.

'Now just a minute!' Mrs Lathom butted in. 'If you're talking about young Harry, he's a really nice, good-hearted lad. He's helped me out many a time. He's certainly no vandal. He shows me a *lot* of respect and he's welcome to come here whenever he likes.'

'Not when we're working here, he's not!' cried Norm. 'I can't be responsible for every kid in the district.'

The argument was promising to warm up into something really big, when the doorbell rang once more and Dez turned up.

'You'll never guess where I've been! Chasing a cheeky young snooper, that's where!'

Breathlessly, Dez outlined the story of his chase. When he mentioned the camera, Norm's eyes narrowed.

'Well you've obviously frightened the lad,' he said thoughtfully. 'Not that he didn't

deserve it! But he can't have gone far. We'd better all get out there and look for him.'

'And just wait till I lay my hands on him!' threatened Mr Bunch.

Meanwhile, up on top of the bedroom bay, Harry lay perfectly still.

'Are you okay?' asked Petra, prodding him in the ribs. 'Because if you are, you'd better start racking your brains. I suppose you realise you've kicked the ladder over? So either we shout for the fire brigade or you come up with a miracle.'

Harry sat up slowly. Why, he was actually alive! His limbs were sound! He was all in one piece! With a bit of luck he could be rescued and start living again. It was almost too good to be true! He didn't fancy the fire brigade idea, though. He could just imagine his dad's reaction if the fire brigade were fetched out for such a purpose.

'I'll think of something in a minute,' he said. 'But did you get some decent photographs? I'm not going through all this for nothing.'

''Course I did! Well, I got one. That's all

we need.'

'Only one? I thought you'd have taken half a dozen at least, just to be on the safe side. Here, give me that camera.' Harry was already looking round for promising shots.

Once Harry became absorbed in his beloved photography he forgot where he was. In fact, if only he had realised it, he seemed to have lost his fear of heights altogether, for there he was, moving quite freely about now on top of the bay window in search of the perfect picture. He took several more photographs of the roof, from as many different angles as he could manage, and one of the pictures included a couple of pigeons perched prettily on the skylight. As he stared at this entrancing scene through his viewfinder he noticed that the skylight was not quite closed. Maybe they could get down that way? After all, the skylight was not more than a couple of arms'-lengths from where he was standing.

He pointed this out excitedly to Petra, but was disappointed when she retorted gloomily: 'You must be joking! Can't you see what a titchy little opening that is? I'd never squeeze through there. I'd get my hips stuck.'

'I could manage it, though!' said Harry, suddenly feeling full of the joys of life. He had just discovered something that he could do and Petra couldn't! There were evidently advantages in being skimpy after all!

7

Mrs Lathom Hears Noises in the Attic

Mrs Lathom's attic was full of dusty junk. In fact, Harry had climbed down into it by way of a scratched old coffee table and a couple of battered travelling trunks which stood providentially one on top of the other right underneath the skylight. (As Petra had prophesied, it had been a tight squeeze through, but an easy climb, compared to that nightmare with the ladder! Harry seemed to be gaining new confidence all the time.)

Harry knew there was a trapdoor in Mrs Lathom's landing ceiling, leading up into the attic. They had a similar one at home. Once he had opened the trapdoor he would be able to attract Mrs Lathom's attention. But he would have to make sure that the old lady was alone. It would never do to have Norm or Dez coming up to fetch him!

Finding the trapdoor was easy, as it was the only patch of floor not covered by junk; but opening it proved to be impossible. Perhaps the woodwork had warped, or perhaps the door was bolted on the outside. Harry could not remember whether he had ever noticed a bolt there or not. He struggled for quite a while, trying desperately to dislodge that trapdoor, but he might as well have saved his strength. At last he climbed back up to the skylight and stuck his head out to give Petra the depressing news.

That was when he realised that it had started raining. This was not gentle rain either, but a really heavy downpour. Poor old Petra was getting soaked and was not very pleased to hear Harry's news.

'Well, bang on the trapdoor!' she yelled impatiently. 'Shout as well. Make as much noise as you can until somebody hears you.'

'Even if it's *them*?'

'Look, do you want me to get washed off

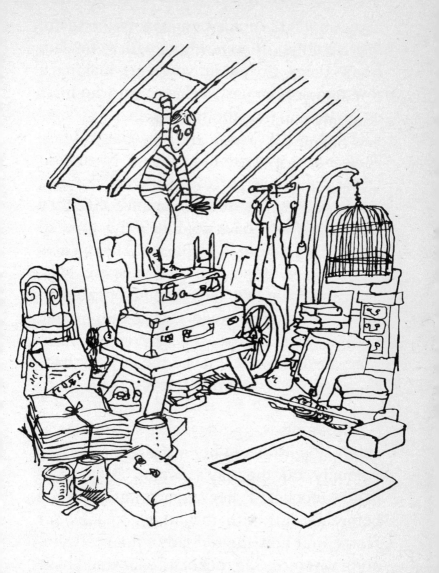

here, or what? In any case it won't be them; they've gone off somewhere with your dad, I saw them. So either you start making a row, or I do. I'm past caring about who finds us, as long as somebody does.'

Harry swiftly considered the possibilities. Now that it was raining so hard, Norm and Dez would have to stop work for the day. So there was a reasonable chance that they wouldn't come back and he'd be able to catch Mrs Lathom in by herself. Harry knew there was a stepladder in the spare back bedroom. The old lady would be able to fetch that, then he could escape with no one else the wiser and set the outside ladder up again for Petra. He'd saved the day! Perhaps he wasn't such a wimp after all.

While all this was going on, Mrs Lathom was sitting downstairs in her armchair, reflecting gloomily on the day's events. Norm had neatly pocketed her money and cheque before he left with the others to look for Harry, and now the old lady's financial situation was dire. She reckoned she would have

to go without the new winter boots she had promised herself; she might even have to cut down on her food and fuel bills. It was all very depressing.

Suddenly she heard a strange noise; hammering or banging. It seemed to be coming from somewhere upstairs. Surely those two hadn't started work on the roof yet? They were supposed to be looking for Harry. Mrs Lathom went over to the window and saw that it had started raining. She also noticed the ladder lying on the ground. Well then, the noise could not be coming from the workmen. Whatever could it be?

At last she went to listen nervously at the foot of the staircase. From there the banging sounded much louder, and now, mixed in with it, there came a suggestion of muffled shouts. The old lady began to feel really scared. After all, these days the newspapers held daily tales of burglaries, muggings and murders. The world had become a frightening place, especially for old ladies living alone. She decided to lock up the house and retreat next door until help could be summoned. Grabbing her coat and handbag, she hurried to the door. Luckily, she was just in time to meet up with Mr Bunch at his garden gate, for when it had started raining so hard the three men had decided to call off their search.

'Well, I won't go in,' decided Jim Bunch

as he listened to Mrs Lathom's tale. 'If you've got intruders the best thing we can do is to telephone the police. They're always warning us not to tackle villains on our own. You come home with me and put the kettle on while I make the call.'

By this time Norm and Dez had piled into their van and driven away. Norm, with the old lady's money safe in his pocket, had the bright idea of keeping going until they reached some remote and distant place where nobody would know them. There they could start work on a new group of victims.

'It might be just as well, seeing we can't be sure what that nosy lad was up to. Pity we couldn't catch up with him.'

Dez said he didn't mind moving on; he was fed up with this area anyway. It had no decent cake shops and only one third-rate chippy which didn't do mushy peas.

They must have travelled at least thirty miles before Dez suddenly slapped his forehead and cried: 'Hey, Norm! We forgot the ladder!'

8

The Photographer Solves the Crime

The police car pulled up at the end of the road, quite a distance away from Mrs Lathom's. Two uniformed officers got out of the car – one man and one woman – and walked along to Harry's house. They were met at the door by Harry's dad who invited them in. Minutes later, the officers crossed to Mrs Lathom's house, used her doorkeys and slipped quietly inside, one by the back door and one by the front.

After that, events speeded up considerably. Harry, who was still yelling and banging in the attic, was relieved to see the trapdoor rising at last. He did not even mind the sight of the police hat rising with it. Rescue had come, and that was all that mattered.

Once they had fetched Petra back down the ladder, the two police officers brought her into Mrs Lathom's house to dry her off. The rain was still cascading down, and Petra certainly was the wettest person Harry had ever seen outside a swimming bath. While the woman was sorting her out with towels and a hair-dryer, Harry told the other officer the tale of Norm and Dez, and their attempts to cheat Mrs Lathom.

Did the policeman believe him? He looked pretty stony-faced, and Harry wondered if the man might think he and Petra were really a couple of burglars, like so many kids these days. Maybe they'd be taken off to the police station – and goodness knew what his dad would say about that!

Then Harry remembered the camera, and the Instamatic photographs, already printed and safe in his pocket. He spread them out eagerly on the table.

'We took these as evidence. See – that's the roof and it certainly isn't falling to bits. And there's a shot of the van! You can see the registration number clear as clingfilm, so you'll soon be able to catch them.' (If they haven't given the van a quick re-spray and changed the registration number, Harry added gloomily to himself.)

The officer picked up the photographs and gave them a cursory glance, but all he said was: 'I think we'd better go and have a word with your dad and Mrs Lathom.'

At the sight of his filthy and bedraggled

son Harry's dad looked ready to explode.

'Now, you look here, my lad - !' he began, but the policeman raised a silencing hand.

'Just a minute, Mr Bunch! Before *you* start chastising the lad, *I've* got a few words to say.' Turning to the children, he went on: 'That was very foolish behaviour, climbing the ladder and cavorting about on the roof. You may think it was clever, but it wasn't. You could both have been killed. And if ever we catch you doing anything like that again, you'll be in serious trouble.'

'You needn't worry,' muttered Harry, 'I wouldn't go up there again for a fortune!'

'No, he wouldn't!' agreed Petra. 'He only went up to rescue me, and he was really brave to do that because he was scared of heights.'

'That's as may be, but next time you need to rescue somebody, call out the emergency services; that's what they're there for.' Suddenly the policeman peered more closely at Petra. 'Here, aren't you the young rascal who climbed up the front of the Town Hall the other week?'

'What if I am? I was only trying to be helpful, *both* times! And since all the climbing was my idea I don't think you should keep going on at Harry. You don't seem to realise he scrambled halfway across the roof to get through the skylight because he knew I couldn't fit through it. If he hadn't done

that, we'd still have been up there. We might have died of exposure before anybody found us. He might not be much in the way of build, but he's the bravest kid I've ever met.'

Harry's mouth fell open with shock. He'd expected trouble, not compliments. But then, it looked as though trouble was what he was going to get from his father.

'That's crazy, not brave!' thundered Mr Bunch. 'You heard what the police officer said? You could both have been killed. And you know very well, our Harry, if I've warned you once about ladders, I've warned you a million times . . .'

'Yes, sir; I'm sure you have,' the policeman butted in. 'And quite right too. But they've had their reprimand now, and before you get too wound up I think you ought to hear *why* they did it.'

Once again Harry told his story – this time backed up by Petra and Mrs Lathom – and once again the photographs were spread out on the table. Mrs Lathom was shocked. She picked up the photographs of the roof and stared at them in disbelief.

'The things they told me about the roof! To hear them talk, it wasn't going to last another month!'

Almost in tears, she explained that she had paid five hundred pounds for its repair.

'Five hundred pounds is a fortune to me, and I'll never see that money again!'

'Well, let's not give up hope just yet,' said the policeman kindly, just as Norm and Dez drove back into the street to collect their ladder.

A few weeks later, when his gran had recovered, his mother was back home again and Norm and Dez were safely in custody awaiting trial, Harry won the coveted Junior Photographer's Trophy with his shot of the pigeons on the skylight. He felt doubly proud, for he knew he would never have managed a shot like that from ground level. It was a once-in-a-lifetime scoop, for in one way of speaking, he would never reach those heights again.

In spite of everything, his mother was proud of him, too. 'Well, our Harry, one way and another you seem to have covered yourself in glory – at least, just about enough of it to gloss over the disgrace.'

She could not help smiling as she served
up generous celebration portions of Ohio
stewed corn to Harry, Petra and Rashid.
'Fancy you squeezing through that poky

little skylight! It just shows what you can do when you eat a proper, sensible diet!' she added wickedly, winking at Harry behind his father's back. 'And haven't I always said it's *pluck* turns you into something big, not food and exercise?'

Mr Bunch grunted uneasily. He had his right arm in a sling, having pulled a muscle at the gym, and was reduced to eating with a spoon. Being too proud to ask for help, he could not very well dine off steaks just yet, as he couldn't cut them up.

'Might as well save me some of that stuff,' he muttered grudgingly, glowering at the corn. 'I might try a bit, just to see how horrible it tastes.'